To my dear little monsters: Ari, Leo and Luca.

Luis Amavisca

*To Leo. This book will always be special
because we created it together.*

Erica Salcedo

The Ugliest Monster in the World
Somos8 Collection

© Text: Luis Amavisca, 2021
© Illustrations: Erica Salcedo, 2021
© Edition: NubeOcho, 2021
www.nubeocho.com · info@nubeocho.com

Text Editing: Rima Noureddine, Rebecca Packard

This book has been typeset in MONST★R characters
by Salvador Figueirido.

First Edition: October 2021
ISBN: 978-84-17673-76-5
Legal Deposit: M-31698-2020

Printed in Portugal.

THE UGLIEST MONSTER IN THE WORLD

Luis Amavisca · Erica Salcedo

nubeOCHO

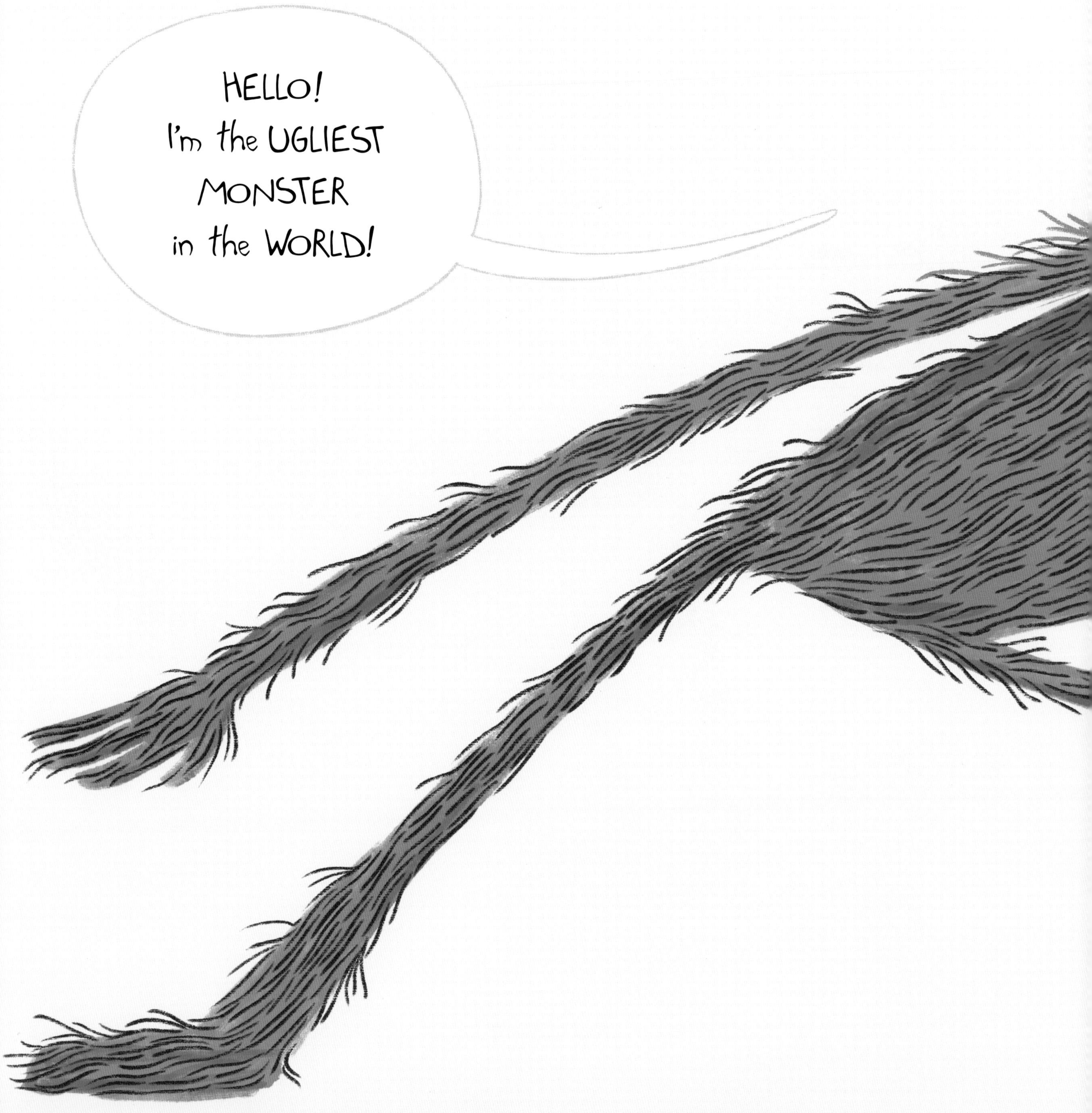
HELLO! I'm the UGLIEST MONSTER in the WORLD!

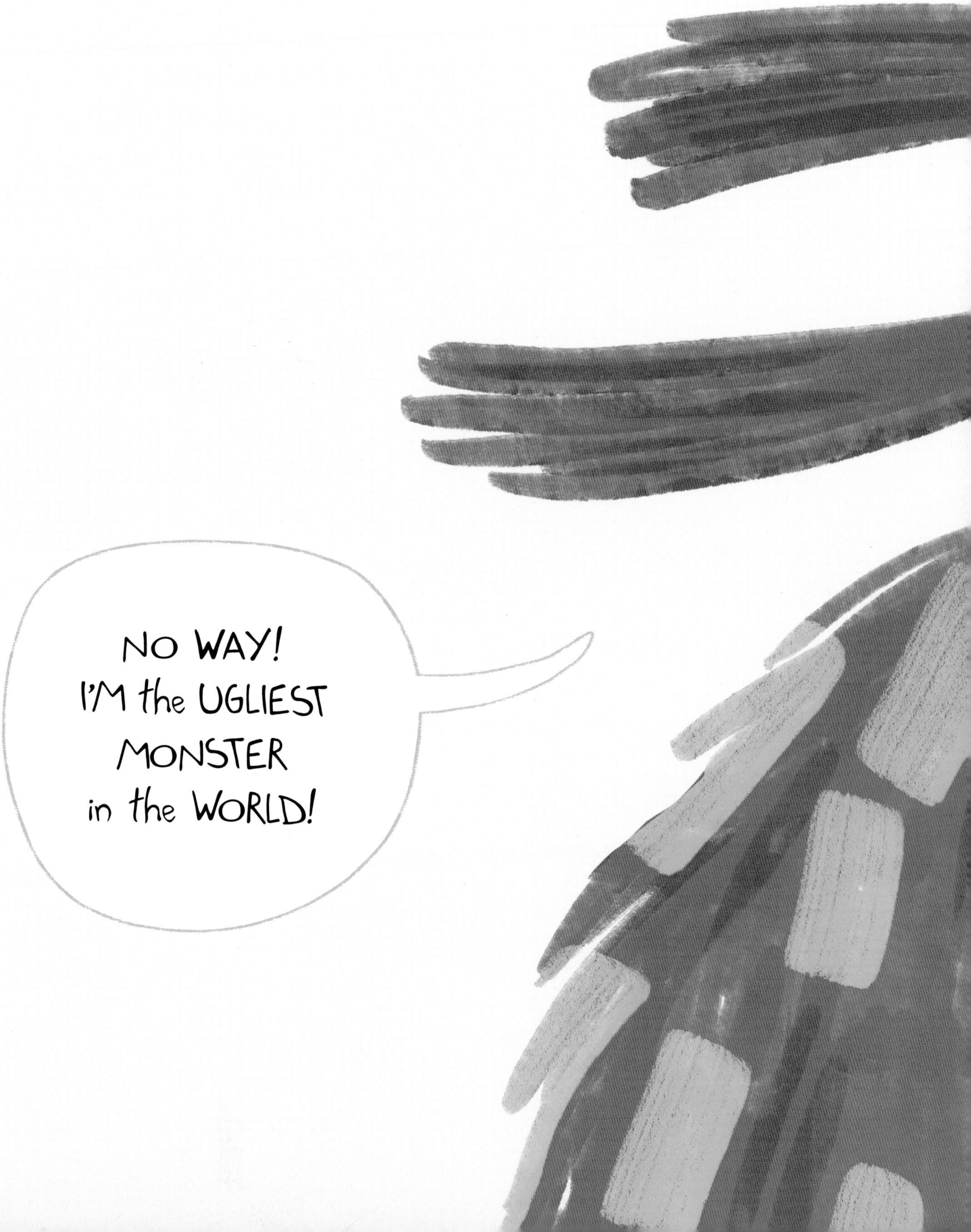
NO WAY!
I'M the UGLIEST
MONSTER
in the WORLD!

Well, you are VERY ugly. But actually... I'M the UGLIEST MONSTER in the WORLD!

PFFFT! That's not true!
Look at these GOOGLY EYES!
And these EYEBROWS!

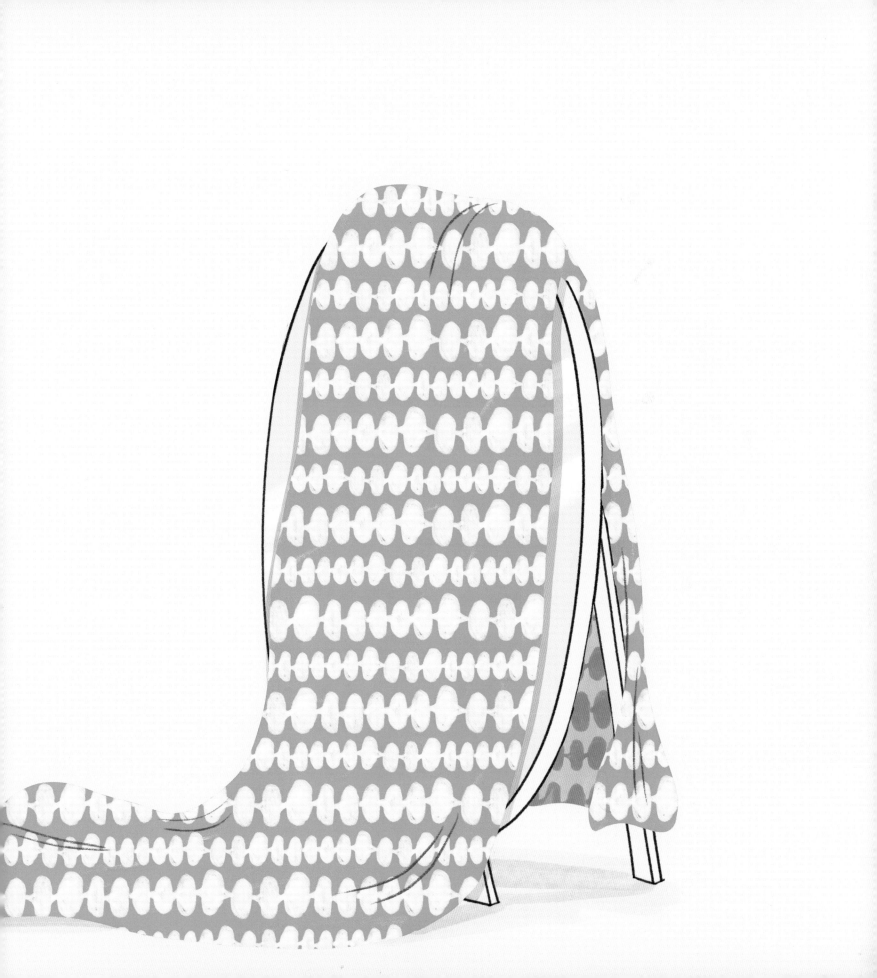

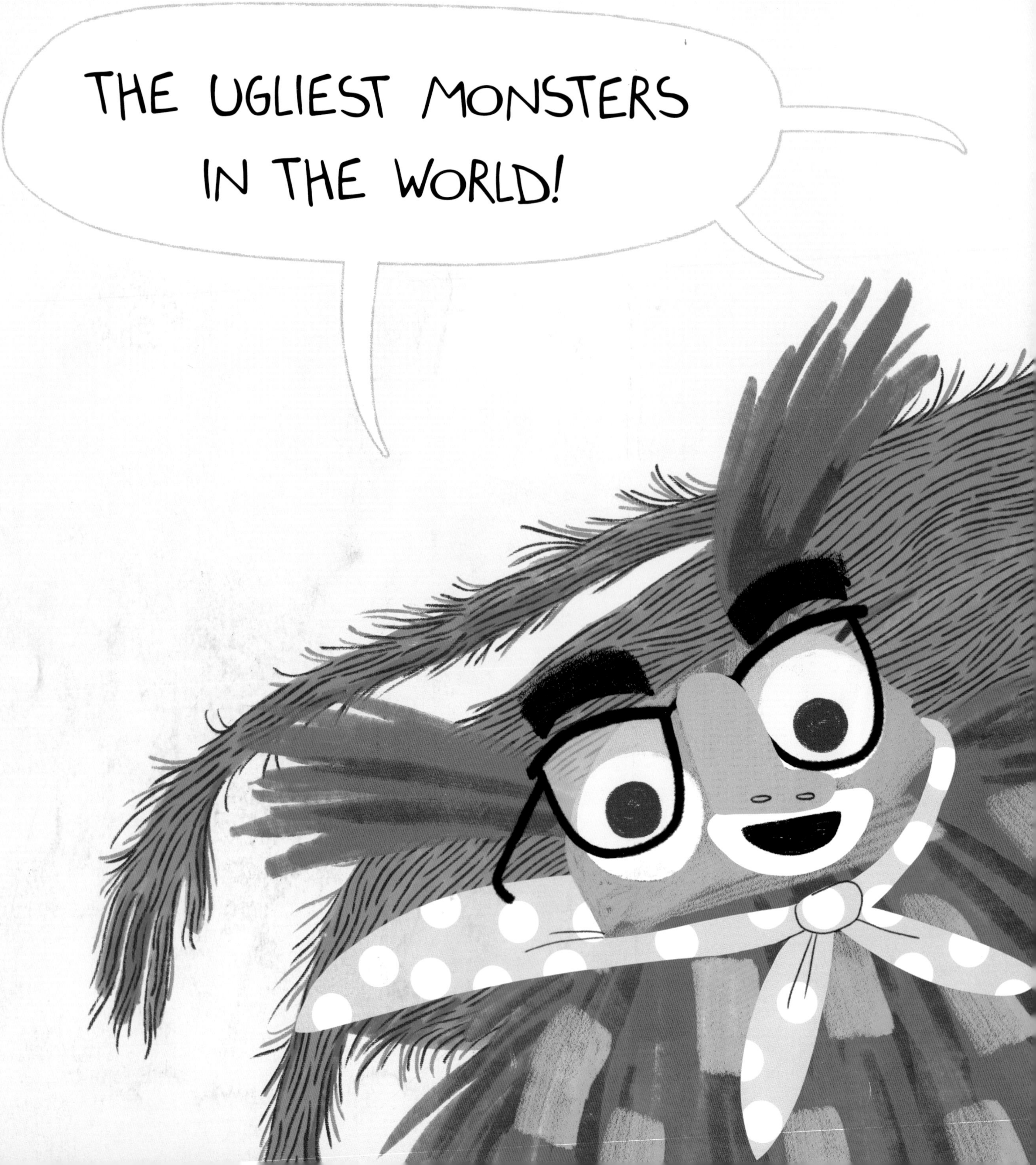
THE UGLIEST MONSTERS IN THE WORLD!